THE WOMAN OF HIS DREAM

Ethel M. Dell

PROLOGUE

It was growing very dark. The decks gleamed wet in the light of the swinging lamps. The wind howled across the sea like a monster in torment. It would be a fearful night.

The man who stood clutching at the slanting deck rail was drenched from head to foot, but, despite this fact, he had no thought of going below. Reginald Carey had been for many voyages on many seas, but the fascination of a storm in the bay attracted him irresistibly still. He had no sympathy with the uneasy crowd in the saloons. He even exulted in the wild tumult of wind and sea and blinding rain. He was as one spellbound in the grip of the tempest.

Curt and dry of speech, abrupt at times almost to rudeness, he was a man of whom most people stood in awe, and with whom very few were on terms of intimacy. Yet in the world of men he had made his mark.

By camp-fires and on the march, in prison and in hospital, Carey the journalist had become a byword for coolness and endurance. It was Carey, caustic of humour, uncompromising of attitude, who sauntered through a hail of bullets to fill a wounded man's water-tin; Carey who pushed his way among stampeding mules to rescue sorely needed medical stores; Carey who had limped beside footsore, jaded men, and whistled them out of their depression.

There were two fingers missing from Carey's left hand, and

the limp had become permanent when he sailed home from South Africa at the end of the war, but he was the personal friend of half the army though there was not a single man who could boast that he knew him thoroughly well. For none knew exactly what this man, who scoffed so freely at disaster, carried in his heart.

As he leaned on the rail of the tossing vessel, gazing steadfastly into the howling darkness, his face was as serene as if he sailed a summer sea. The great waves that dashed their foam over him as he stood were powerless to raise fear in his soul! He stood as one apart—a lonely watcher whom no danger could appal.

It was growing late, but he took no count of time. More than once he had been hoarsely advised to go below, but he would not go. He believed himself to be the only passenger on deck, and he clung to his solitude. The bare thought of the stuffy saloon was abhorrent to him. He marvelled that no one else had developed the same distaste.

And with the thought he turned, breathless from the buffeting spray of a mighty wave, to find a woman standing near him on the swirling deck.

She stood poised lightly as a bird prepared for flight, her head bare, her face upturned to the storm. Her hands were fast gripped upon the rail, and the gleam of a gold ring caught Carey's eye. He saw that she was unconscious of his presence. The shifting, uncertain light had not revealed him. For a space he stood watching her, unperceived, wondering at the courage that upheld her. Her hair had blown loose in the wind, and lay in a black mass upon her neck. He could not see her features, but her bearing was superb.

And then at length, as if his quiet scrutiny had somehow touched in her a responsive chord, she turned her head and saw him. Their eyes met, and a curious thrill ran tingling through the man's veins. He had never seen this woman before, but as she looked at him, with wonderful dark eyes that seemed to hold a passionate exultation in their depths, he suddenly felt as if he had known her all his life. They were comrades. It was no hysterical panic that had driven her up from below.

Like himself, she had
been drawn by the
magic of the storm.

Impulsively, almost
involuntarily, he
moved a pace towards
her and stretched
out a hand along the
dripping rail.

She gave him her
own instantly
and confidently,
responding to his
action with absolute

simplicity. It was a gesture of sympathy, of fellowship. She bore herself as a queen, but she did not condescend to him.

No words passed between them. Both realised the impossibility of speech in that shrieking tempest. Moreover, there was no need for speech. Earth's petty conventions had fallen

away from them.
They were as children
standing hand in hand
on the edge of the
unknown, hearing
the same thunderous
music, bound by the
same magic spell.

Carey wondered
later how long a time
elapsed whilst they
stood thus, intently
watching. It might
have been for merely
a few minutes, or it

might have been for
the greater part of an
hour. He never knew.

The spell broke at
length suddenly
and terribly, with a
grinding crash that
flung them both
sideways upon the
slippery deck. He
went down, still
clinging instinctively
to the rail, and the
next instant, by its
aid, he was on his feet

again, dragging his companion up with him.

There followed a pause—a shuddering, expectant pause— while wind and sea raged all around them like beasts of prey. And through it there came the sound of the engine throbbing impotently spasmodically, like the heart of a dying man. Quite suddenly it ceased, and there was a frightful uproar of escaping steam. The deck on which they stood began to tilt slowly upwards.

Carey knew what had happened. They had struck a rock in that awful darkness, and they were going down with frightful rapidity into the seething, storm-tossed water.

He had never been shipwrecked before, but, as by instinct, he realised the madness of remaining where he was. A coil of rope lay almost at his feet, and he stooped and seized it. There had come a brief lull in the storm, but he knew that there was not a moment to spare. Still supporting his companion, he began to bind the rope around them both.

She looked up at him quickly, and he saw her lips move in protest. She even set her hands against his breast, as if to resist him. But he overcame her almost savagely. It was no moment for argument.

The slope of the deck was becoming every

instant more acute. The wind was racing back across the sea. Above them—very far above them, it seemed—there was a confusion of figures, but the tumult of wind and waves drowned all other sound. Carey's feet began to slip on that awful slant. They were sinking rapidly, rapidly.

He knotted the rope and gathered himself together. An instant he hung on the rail, breathing deeply. Then with a jerk he relaxed his grip and leaped blindly into the howling darkness, hurling himself and the woman with him far into the raging sea.

It was suffocatingly hot. Carey raised his

arms with a desperate movement. He felt as if he were swimming in hot vapour. And he had been swimming for a long time, too. He was deadly tired. A light flashed in his eyes, and very far above him—like an object viewed through the small end of a telescope—he saw a face. Vaguely he heard a voice speaking, but what

it said was beyond
his comprehension.
It seemed to
utter unintelligible
things. For a while
he laboured to
understand, then the
effort became too
much for him. The
light faded from his
brain.

Later—much later, it
seemed—he awoke
to full consciousness,
to find himself in a

Breton fisherman's cottage, watched over by a kindly little French doctor who tended him as though he had been his brother.

"Monsieur is better, but much better," he was cheerily assured. "And for madame his wife he need have no inquietude. She is safe and well, and only concerns herself for monsieur."

This was reassuring, and Carey accepted it without comment or inquiry. He knew that there was a misunderstanding somewhere, but he was still too exhausted to trouble himself about so slight a matter. He thanked his kindly informant, and again he slept.

Two days later
his interest in life
revived. He began to
ask questions, and
received from the
doctor a full account
of what had occurred.

He had been washed
ashore, he was told—
he and madame his
wife—lashed fast
together. The ship
had been wrecked
within half a mile
of the land. But the

seas had been terrific. There had not been many survivors.

Carey digested the news in silence. He had had no friends on board, having embarked only at Gibraltar.

At length he looked up with a faint smile at his faithful attendant. "And where is— madame?" he asked.

The little doctor hesitated, and spread out his hands deprecatingly.

"Oh, monsieur, I regret—I much regret—to have to inform you that she is already departed for Paris. Her solicitude for you was great, was pathetic. The first words she speak were: 'My husband, do not let him know!'

as though she feared
that you would be
distressed for her.
And then she recover
quick, quick, and say
that she must go—
that monsieur when he
know, will understand.
And so she depart
early in the morning
of yesterday while
monsieur is still
asleep."

He was watching
Carey with obvious

anxiety as he ended, but the Englishman's face expressed nothing but a somewhat elaborate indifference.

"I see," he said, and relapsed into silence.

He made no further reference to the matter, and the doctor discreetly abstained from asking questions.

He presently showed him an English paper which contained the information that Mr. and Mrs. Carey were among the rescued.

"That," he remarked, "will alleviate the anxiety of your friends."

To which Carey responded, with a curt laugh: "No one knew that we were on board."

He left for Paris on the following day, allowing the doctor to infer that he was on his way to join his wife.

I

It was growing dark in the empty class-room, but there was nothing left to do, and the French mistress, sitting alone at her high desk, made no move to turn on the light. All the lesson books were packed away out of sight. There was not so much as a stray pencil trespassing upon that desert of orderliness. Only the waste-paper basket, standing behind Mademoiselle Trèves's chair, gave evidence of the tempest of energy that had preceded this empty calm in the midst of which she sat alone. It was crammed to overflowing with torn exercise books, and all manner of schoolgirls' rubbish, and now and then it creaked eerily in the desolate silence as though at the touch of an invisible hand.

It was very cold in the great room, for the fire had gone out long ago. There was no one left to enjoy it except mademoiselle, who apparently did not count. For most of the pupils had departed in the morning, and those who were left were collected in the great hall speeding one after another upon their homeward way. All day the wheels of cabs had crunched the gravel below the class-room window, but they were not so audible now, for the ground was thickly covered with snow, which had been drearily falling throughout the afternoon.

It lay piled upon the window-sill, casting a ghostly light into the darkening room, vaguely outlining the slender figure that sat so still before the high desk.

Another cab-load of laughing girls was just passing out at the gate. There could not be many left. The darkness increased, and mademoiselle drew a quick breath and shivered. She wished the departures were all over.

There came a light step in the passage, and a daring whistle, which broke off short as a hand impetuously opened the class-room door.

"Why, mademoiselle!" cried a fresh young voice. "Why, chérie!" Warm arms encircled the lonely figure, and eager lips pressed the cold face. "Oh, chérie, don't grizzle!" besought the newcomer. "Why, I've never known you do such a thing before. Have you been here all this time? I've been looking for you all over the place. I couldn't leave without one more good-bye. And see here, chérie, you must—you must—come to my birthday-party on New Year's Eve. If you won't come and

stay with me, which
I do think you might,
you must come down
for that one night.
It's no distance, you
know. And it's only
a children's show.
There won't be any
grown-ups except
my cousin Reggie,
who is the sweetest
man in the world, and
Mummy's Admiral who
comes next. Say you
will, chérie, for I shall
be sixteen—just think

of it!—and I do want you to be there. You will, won't you? Come, promise!"

It was hard
to refuse this
petitioner, so warmly
fascinating was she.
Mademoiselle, who,
it was well known,
never accepted any
invitations, hesitated
for the first time—and
was lost.

"If I came just for that one evening then, Gwen, you would not press me to stay longer?"

"Bless you, no!" declared Gwen. "I'll drive you to the station myself in Mummy's car to catch the first train next morning, if you'll come. And I'll make Reggie come too. You'll just love

Reggie, chérie. He's my exact ideal of what a man ought to be—the best friend I have, next to you. Well, it's a bargain then, isn't it? You'll come and help dance with the kids—you promise? That's my own sweet chérie! And now you mustn't grizzle here in the dark any longer. I believe my cab is at the door. Come down and see me off, won't you?"

Yet again she was irresistible. They went out together, hand in hand, happy child and lonely woman, and the door of the deserted class-room banged with a desolate echoing behind them.

II

It was ten days later, on a foggy evening, in the end of the year, that Reginald Carey alighted at a small wayside station, and grimly prepared himself for a five-mile trudge through dark and muddy lanes to his destination.

The only conveyance in the station yard

was a private motor car, and his first glance at this convinced him that it was not there to await him. He paused under the lamp outside to turn up his collar, and, as he did so, a man of gigantic breadth and stature, wearing goggles, came out of the station behind him and strode past. He glanced at Carey casually as he went by, looked again, then suddenly stopped and peered at him.

"Great Scotland!" he exclaimed abruptly. "I know you—or ought to. You're the little newspaper chap who saved my life at Magersfontein. Thought there was something familiar about you the moment I saw you. You remember me, eh?"

He turned back his goggles impetuously, and showed Carey his face.

Yes; Carey remembered him very well indeed, though he was not sure that the acquaintance was one he desired to improve. He took the proffered hand with a certain reserve.

"Yes; I remember you. I don't think I ever heard your name, but that's a detail. You came out of it all right, then?"

"Oh, yes; more or less. Nothing ever hurts me." The big man's laugh had in it a touch of bitterness. "Where are you bound for? Come along with me in the car; I'll take you where you want to go." He seized Carey by the shoulder, impelling him with boisterous cordiality towards the vehicle. "Jump in, my friend. My name is Coningsby— Major Coningsby, of Crooklands Manor— mad Coningsby I'm called about here, because I happen to ride straighter to hounds than most of 'em. A bit of a compliment, eh? But they're a shocking set of muffs in these parts. You don't live here?"

"No; I am down on a visit to my cousin, Lady Emberdale. She lives at Crooklands Mead. I've come down a day sooner than I was expected, and the train was two hours late. I'm Reginald Carey." He stopped before the step of the car. "It's very good of you, but I won't take you out of your way on such a beastly night. I can quite well walk."

"Nonsense, man! It's no distance, and it isn't out of the way. I've only just motored down to get an evening paper. You're just in time to dine with me. I'm all alone, and confoundedly glad to see you. I know Lady Emberdale well. Come, jump in!"

Thus urged, Carey yielded, not over-willingly, and took his seat in the car.

Directly they started, he knew the reason for his companion's pseudonym, for they whizzed out of the yard at a speed which

must have disquieted
the stoutest nerves.

It was the maddest
ride he had ever
experienced, and
he wondered by
what instinct Major
Coningsby kept
a straight course
through the darkness.
Their own lamps
provided the only
light there was, and
when they presently
turned sharply

at right angles he gathered himself together instinctively in preparation for a smash.

But nothing happened. They tore on a little farther in darkness, travelling along a private road; and then the lights of a house pierced the gloom.

Coningsby brought his car to a standstill.

"Tumble out! The front door is straight ahead. My man will let you in and look after you. Excuse me a moment while I take the car round!"

He was gone with the words, leaving Carey to ascend a flight of steps to the hall door. It opened at once to admit him, and he found himself in a great hall dimly illumined by firelight. A servant helped him to divest himself of his overcoat, and silently led the way.

The room he entered was furnished as a library. He glanced round it as he stood on the hearth-rug, awaiting his host, and was chiefly struck by the general atmosphere of dreariness that pervaded it. Its sombre oak furniture seemed to absorb instead of reflecting the light. There was a large oil-painting above the fireplace, and after a few seconds he turned his head and saw it. It was the portrait of a woman.

Young, beautiful, queenly, the painted face looked down

into his own, and the man's heart gave a sudden, curious throb that was half rapture and half pain. In a moment the room he had just entered, with all the circumstances that had taken him there, was blotted from his brain. He was standing once more on the rocking deck of a steamer, in a tempest of wind and rain and furious sea, facing the storm, exultant, with a woman's hand fast gripped in his.

"Are you looking at that picture?" said a voice. "It's my wife—dead now—lost—five years ago—at sea!"

Carey wheeled sharply at the jerky utterance. Coningsby was standing by his side. He was staring upwards at the portrait, a strange gleam darting in his eyes—a gleam not wholly sane.

"It doesn't do her justice," he went on in the same abrupt, headlong fashion. "But it's better than nothing. She was the only woman who ever satisfied me. Her loss damaged me badly. I've never been the same since.

There've been others, of course, but she was always first—an easy first. I shall want her—I shall go on wanting her—till I'm in my grave." His voice was suddenly husky, as the voice of a man in pain. "It's like a fiery thirst," he said. "I try to quench it—Heaven knows I try! But it comes back—it comes back."

He swung round on his heel and went to the table. There followed the clink of glasses, but Carey did not turn. His eyes had left the picture, and were fixed, stern and unwinking, upon the fire that glowed at his feet.

Again he seemed to feel the clasp of a woman's hand, free and confiding, within his own. Again his heart stirred responsively in the quick warmth of a woman's perfect sympathy.

And he knew that into his keeping had been given the secret of that woman's existence. The five years' mystery was solved at last. He understood, and, understanding, he

kept silent faith with
her.

III

It was two hours later
that Carey presented
himself at his cousin's
house. He entered
unobtrusively, as his
manner was, knowing
himself to be a
welcome guest.

The first person to

greet him was Gwen, who, accompanied by a college youth of twenty, was roasting chestnuts in front of the hall fire. She sprang up at the sound of his voice, and, flushed and eager, rushed to meet him.

"Why, Reggie, my dear old boy, who would have thought of seeing you to-night?

Come right in! Aren't you very cold? How did you get here? Have you dined? This is Charlie Rivers, the Admiral's son. Charlie, you have heard me speak of my cousin, Mr. Carey."

Charlie had, several times over, and said so, with a grin, as he made room for Carey in front of the blaze, taking care to keep himself next to Gwen.

Carey considerately
fell in with the
manoeuvre and,
greetings over, they
huddled sociably
together over
the fire, and fell
to discussing the
birthday party which
was to be held on the
morrow.

Gwen was a curious
blend of excitement

and common sense. She had been busily preparing all day for the coming festivity.

"There's one visitor I want you both to be very good to," she said, "and see that she takes plenty of refreshments, whether she wants them or not."

Young Rivers grimaced at Carey.

"You can have my share of this unattractive female," he said generously. "It's Gwen's schoolmistress, and I'll bet she's as heavy as a sack of coals."

"I can't dance. I'm lame," said Carey. "But I don't mind sitting out in the refreshment room to please Gwen. How old is she, Gwen? About twice my age?"

Gwen did not stop to calculate.

"Older than that, I should think. Her hair is quite grey, and she's very sad and quiet. I am sure she has had a lot of trouble. Very likely she won't want to dance either, so there will be a pair of you. Her name is

Mademoiselle Trèves, but she is only half French, and speaks English better than I do. She never goes anywhere, so I do want her to have a good time. You will be kind to her, won't you? I'll introduce you to her as early as possible. We are all going to wear masks till midnight."

"Stupid

things—masks," said Charlie very decidedly. "Don't like 'em."

Gwen turned upon him.

"It's much the fairest way. If we didn't wear them, the pretty girls would get all the best dances."

"Oh, well, you wouldn't be left out, anyway," he assured

her.

At which compliment
Gwen sniffed
contemptuously, and
pointedly requested
Carey to give her a
few minutes in strict
privacy before they
parted for the night.

He saw that she
meant it; and
when Charlie had
reluctantly taken
himself off he went

with his young cousin to her own little sitting-room upstairs before seeking Lady Emberdale in the drawing-room.

Gwen could scarcely wait till the door was closed before she began to lay her troubles before him.

"It's Mummy!" she told him very seriously. "You can't think how sick and disgusted I am. Sit down, Reggie, and I'll tell you all about it! Being Mummy's trustee, perhaps you will have some influence over her. I have none. She thinks I'm prejudiced. And I'm not, Reggie. There's nothing to make me so except that Charlie is a nice boy, and the Admiral a perfect darling." She paused for breath, and Carey patiently waited for further enlightenment. It came.

"Of course," she said, seating herself on the arm of his chair, "I've always known that Mummy would marry again some day or other. She's so young and pretty; and I haven't minded the idea a bit. Poor, dear Dad was always such a very, very old man! But I do want her to marry someone nice now the time has come. All through the summer holidays I felt sure it was going to be the Admiral, and I was so pleased about it. Charlie and I used to make bets about its coming off before Christmas. He was ever so pleased, too, and we'd settled to join together for the wedding present so as to get something decent. It was all going to be so jolly. And now," with a great sigh, "everything's spoilt. There's— there's someone else."

"Good heavens!" said Carey. "Who?"

He had been suppressing a laugh during the greater part of Gwen's confidence, but this last announcement startled him into sobriety. A very faint misgiving stirred in his soul. What if—but no; it was preposterous. He thrust it from him.

Gwen slid a loving arm about his neck.

"I like telling you things, Reggie. You always understand,

and they never worry me so much afterwards. For I am—horribly worried. Mummy met him in the hunting field. He has come to live quite near us—oh, such a brute he is, loud and coarse and bullying! He rode a horse to death only a few weeks ago. They say he's mad, and I'm nearly sure he drinks as well.

And he and Mummy
have chummed up.
They are as thick
as thieves, and he's
always coming to the
house, dropping in at
odd hours. The poor,
dear Admiral hasn't
a chance. He's much
too gentlemanly to
elbow his way in
like—like this horrid
Major Coningsby. Oh,
Reggie, do you think
you can do anything
to stop it? I don't

want her to marry him, neither does Charlie. My, Reggie, what's the matter? You don't know him, do you? You don't know anything bad about him?"

Carey was on his feet, pacing slowly to and fro. One hand—the maimed left hand—was thrust away out of sight, as his habit was in a woman's presence. The other was clenched hard at his side.

He did not at once answer Gwen's agitated questioning. She sat and watched him in some anxiety, wondering at the stern perplexity with which he reviewed the problem.

Suddenly he stopped in front of her.

"Yes; I know the man," he said. "I knew him years ago in South Africa, and I met him again to-night. I must think this matter over, and consider it carefully. You are quite sure of what you say—quite sure he is attracted by your mother?"

Gwen nodded.

"Oh, there's no doubt

of that. He treats her already as if she were his property. You won't tell her I told you, Reggie? It will simply precipitate matters if you do."

"No; I shan't tell her. I never argue with women." Carey spoke almost savagely. He was staring at something that Gwen could not see.

"Do you think you will be able to stop it?" she asked him, with a slightly nervous hesitation.

His eyes came back to her. He seemed to consider her for a moment. Then, seeing that she was really troubled, he spoke with sudden kindliness:

"I think so, yes. But

never mind how! Leave it to me and put it out of your head as much as possible! I quite agree with you that it is an arrangement that wouldn't do at all. Why on earth couldn't your friend the Admiral speak before?"

"I wish he had," said Gwen, from her heart. "And I

believe he does, too, now. But men are so idiotic, Reggie. They always miss their opportunities."

"Think so?" said Carey. "Some men never have any, it seems to me."

And he left her wondering at the bitterness of his speech.

IV

The winter sunlight
was streaming into
Major Coningsby's
gloomy library when
Carey again stood
within it. The Major
was out riding, he
had been told, but he
was expected back
ere long; and he had
decided to wait for
him.

And so he stood waiting before the portrait; and closely, critically, he studied it by the morning light.

It was the face which for five years now he had carried graven on his heart. She was the one woman to him—the woman of his dream. Throughout his wanderings he had cherished the memory of her—a secret and

priceless possession
to which he clung day
and night, waking
and sleeping. He had
made no effort to
find her during those
years, but silently,
almost in spite of
himself, he had kept
her in his heart, had
called her to him in
his dreams, yearning
to her across the
ever-widening gulf,
hungering dumbly
for the voice he had

never heard.

He knew that he was no favourite with women. All his life his reserve had been a barrier that none had ever sought to pass till this woman—the woman who should have been his fate— had been drifted to him through life's stress and tumult and had laid her hand with perfect confidence in his. And now it was laid upon him to betray that confidence. He no longer had the right to keep her secret. He had protected her once, and it had been as a hidden, sacred bond invisibly linking them together. But it could do so no longer. The time had come to wrest that precious link apart.

Sharply he turned from the picture. The dark eyes tortured him. They seemed to be pleading with him, entreating him. There came a sudden clatter without, the tramp of heavy feet, the jingle of spurs. The door was flung noisily back, and Major Coningsby strode in.

"Hullo! Very good of you to look me up so

soon. Sorry I wasn't in to receive you. Haven't you had a drink yet?"

He tossed his riding-whip down upon the table, and busied himself with the glasses.

Carey drew near; his face was stern.

"I have something to say to you," he

said, "before we drink, if you have no objection."

His voice was quiet and very even, but Coningsby looked up with a quick frown.

"Confound you, Carey! What are you pulling a long face about this time of the morning? Better have a drink; it'll make you feel more sociable."

He spoke with sharp irritation. The hand that held the spirit-decanter was not over-steady. Carey watched him—coldly critical.

"That portrait over the mantelpiece," he said; "your wife, I think you told me?"

Coningsby swore a deep oath.

"I may have told you so. I don't often mention the subject. She is dead."

"I beg your pardon; I am forced to mention it." Carey's tone was deliberate, emotionless, hard. "That lady—the original of that portrait—is still alive, to the best of my belief. At least, she was not lost at sea on the occasion of the wreck of the Denver Castle five years ago."

"What?" said Coningsby. He turned suddenly white—white to the lips, and set down the decanter he was still holding as if he had been struck powerless. "What?" he said again, with starting eyes upon

Carey's face.

"I think you understood me," Carey returned coldly. "I have told you because, upon consideration, it seemed to me you ought to know."

The thing was done and past recall, but deep in his heart there lurked a savage resentment against

this man who had
forced him to break
his silence. He felt no
sympathy with him;
he only knew disgust.

Coningsby moved
suddenly with a
frantic oath, and
gripped him by the
shoulder. The blood
was coming back
to his face in livid
patches; his eyes
were terrible.

"Go on!" he said thickly. "Out with it! Tell me all you know!"

He towered over Carey. There was violence in his grip, but Carey did not seem to notice. He faced the giant with absolute composure.

"I can tell you no more," he said. "I knew she was saved, because I was saved with her. But she left Brittany while I was still too ill to move."

"You must know more than that!" shouted Coningsby, losing all control of himself, and shaking his informant furiously by the shoulder. "If she was saved, how did she come to be reported missing?"

For a single instant

Carey hesitated; then, with steady eyes upon the bloated face above him, he made quiet reply:

"Her name was among the missing by her own contrivance. Doubtless she had her reasons."

Coningsby's face suddenly changed: his eyes shone red.

"You helped her!" he snarled, and lifted a clenched fist.

Carey's maimed hand came quietly into view, and closed upon the man's wrist.

"It is not my custom," he coldly said, "to refuse help to a woman."

"Confound you!" stormed Coningsby.

"Where is she now? Where? Where?"

There fell a sudden pause. Carey's eyes were like steel; his grasp never slackened.

"If I knew," he said deliberately, at length, "I should not tell you! You are not fit for the society of any good woman."

The words fell keen as a whip-lash, and as pitiless. Coningsby glared into his face like a goaded bull; his look was murderous. And then by some chance his eyes fell upon the hand that gripped his wrist. He looked at it closely, attentively, for a few seconds, and finally set Carey free.

"You may thank

that," he said more quietly, "for getting you out of the hottest corner you were ever in. I didn't notice it yesterday, though I remember now that you were wounded. So you parted with half your hand to drag me out of that hell, did you? It was a rank, bad investment on your part."

He flung away

abruptly, and helped himself to some brandy. A considerable pause ensued before he spoke again.

"Egad!" he said then, with a harsh laugh, "it's a deuced ingenious lie, this of yours. I suppose you and that imp of mischief, Gwen, hatched it up between you? I saw she had got her thinking-cap on yesterday. I am not considered good enough for her lady mother. But, mark you, I'm going to have her for all that! It isn't good for man to live alone, and I have taken a fancy to Evelyn Emberdale."

"You don't believe me?" Carey asked.

Somehow, though he

had been prepared for bluster and even violence, he had not expected incredulity.

Coningsby filled and emptied his glass a second time before he answered.

"No," he said then, with sudden savagery: "I don't believe you! You had better get out of my house at once, or—I warn you—I may break every bone in your blackguardly body yet!" He turned on Carey, leaping madness in his eyes.

But Carey stood like a rock. "You know the truth," he said quietly.

Coningsby broke into another wild laugh, and pointed up at the picture above his head.

"I shall know it," he declared, "when the sea gives up its dead. Till that day I am free to console myself in my own way, and no one shall stop me."

"You are not free," Carey said. Very steadily he faced the man, very distinctly he spoke. "And, however you console yourself, it will not be with my cousin Lady

Emberdale."

Coningsby turned back to the table to fill his glass again. He spilt the spirit over the cloth as he did it.

"Man alive," he gibed, "do you think she will believe you if I don't?"

It was the weak point of his position, and Carey realised it. It was more than probable that Lady Emberdale would take Coningsby's view of the matter. If the man really attracted her it was almost a foregone conclusion. He knew Gwen's mother well—her inconsequent whims, her obstinacy.

Yet, even in face of this check, he stood his ground.

"I may find some means of proving what I have told you," he said, with unswerving resolution.

Coningsby drained his glass for the third time, and, with a menacing sweep of the hand, seized his riding-whip.

"I don't advise you to come here with your proofs," he snarled.

"The only proof I would look at is the woman herself. Now, sir, I have warned you fairly. Are you going?"

His attitude was openly threatening, but Carey's eyes were piercingly upon him, and, in spite of himself, he paused. So for the passage of seconds they stood; then slowly Carey turned away.

"I am going," he said, "to find your wife."

He did not glance again at the picture as he passed from the room. He could not bring himself to meet the dark eyes that followed him.

V

Yes; he would find her. But how? There was only one course open to him, and he shrank from that with disgust unutterable. It was useless to think of advertising. He was convinced that she would never answer an advertisement.

The only way to find her was to employ

a detective to track her down. He clenched his hands in impotent revolt. Not only had it been laid upon him to betray her confidence, but he must follow this up by dragging her from her hiding-place, and returning her to the bitter bondage from which he had once helped her to escape.

That she still lived

he was inwardly convinced. He would have given all he had to have known her dead.

But, for that day, at least, there was no more to be done, and Gwen must not have her birthday spoilt by the knowledge of his failure. He decided to keep out of her way till the evening.

When he entered the ball-room at the appointed time she pounced upon him eagerly, but her young guests were nearly all assembled, and it was no moment for private conversation.

"Oh, Reggie! There you are! How dreadful you look in a mask! This is my cousin, mademoiselle," turning to a lady in black who accompanied her. "I've been wanting to introduce him to you. Don't forget that the masks are not to come off till midnight. We're going to boom the big gong when the clock strikes twelve."

She flitted away in her shimmering fairy's dress, closely attended by Charlie Rivers, to persuade his father to give her a dance. The room was crowded with masked guests, Lady Emberdale, handsome and brilliant, and Admiral Rivers, her bluff but faithful admirer, being the only exceptions to the rule of the evening.

Carey found himself standing apart with Gwen's particular protégée, and he realised at once that he could expect no help from Charlie in this quarter. For, though slim and graceful, Mademoiselle Trèves's general appearance was undeniably sombre and elderly. The hair that she wore coiled regally upon her head was silver-grey, and there was a certain weariness about the mouth that, though it did not rob it of its sweetness, deprived it of all suggestion of youth.

"I don't know if I am justified in asking for a dance," Carey said. "My own dancing days are over."

She smiled at him, and instantly the weariness vanished. There was magic in her smile.

"I am no dancer either, except with the little ones. If you care to sit out with me, I shall be very pleased."

Her voice was low and musical. It caught his fancy so that he was aware of a sudden curiosity to see the face that the black mask concealed.

"Give me the

twelve-o'clock dance," he said, "if you can spare it!"

She consulted the programme that hung from her wrist. He bent over it as she held it, and scrawled his initials against the dance in question.

"Perhaps I shall not stay for that one," she said, with slight hesitation.

He glanced up at her.

"I thought you were here for the night."

She bent her head.

"But I may slip away before twelve for all that."

Carey smiled.

"I don't think you will, not anyhow if I have a voice in the matter. I am Gwen's lieutenant, you know, specially enrolled to prevent any deserting. There is a heavy penalty for desertion."

"What is it?"

Carey bent again over the programme.

"Deserters will be brought back ignominiously and made to dance with everyone in the room in turn."

He glanced up again at the sound of her low laugh. There was something elusively suggestive about her personality.

"May I have another?" he said. "I hope you don't mind holding the card for me."

"You have hurt your

hand?" she asked.

It was thrust away, as usual, in his pocket.

"Some years ago," he told her. "I don't use it more than I can help."

"How disagreeable for you!" she murmured.

He shrugged his shoulders.

"I am used to it. It

is worse for others than it is for me. May I have No. 9? It includes the supper interval. Thanks! And any more you can spare. I'm only lounging about and seeing that the kids enjoy themselves. I shall be delighted to sit out with you when you are tired of dancing."

"You are very kind,"

she said.

He made her an abrupt bow.

"Then I hope you won't snub my efforts by deserting?"

She laughed again.

"No, lieutenant, I will not desert. I am going to help you."

She spoke with a

winning and impulsive graciousness that stirred again within him that curious sense of groping in the dark among objects familiar but unrecognisable. Surely he had met this stranger somewhere before—in a crowded thoroughfare, in a train, possibly in a theatre, or even in a church!

She looked at him questioningly as he lingered, and with another bow he turned and left her. Doubtless, when he saw her face he would remember, or realise that he had been mistaken.

VI

Mademoiselle Trèves kept her word, and

wherever the fun was at its height she was invariably the centre of it. The shy children crowded about her. She seemed to possess a special charm for them.

Gwen was delighted, and was obviously enjoying herself to the utmost. In the absence of her bête noire whom she had courageously omitted to invite, she rejoiced to see that her mother was being unusually gracious to her beloved Admiral, who was as merry as a schoolboy in consequence.

She was shrewdly aware, however, that the welcome change was but temporary. Incomprehensible though it was to Gwen, she knew that

Major Coningsby's power over her gay and frivolous young mother was absolute. He ruled her with a rod of iron, and Lady Emberdale actually enjoyed his tyranny. The rough court he paid her served to turn her head completely, and she never attempted to resist his influence.

It was all very

distasteful to Gwen, who hated the man with the whole force of her nature. She was thankful to feel that Carey was enlisted on her side. She looked upon him as a tower of strength, and, forebodings notwithstanding, she was able to throw herself heart and soul into the evening's festivities, and to beam delightedly upon her cousin as she walked behind him with Charlie to the supper room.

Carey was escorting the French governess. He found a comfortable corner for her in the thronged room at a table laid for two.

"I am bearing in mind your promise to stand by till twelve

o'clock," he said. "It's the only thing that keeps me going, for I have a powerful longing to remove my mask in defiance of orders. It feels like a porous plaster. I shall only hold out till midnight with your gallant assistance."

He stooped with the words to pick up her fan which she had dropped. He was obliged to use his left hand, and he knew that she gave a quick start at sight of it. But she spoke instantly and he admired her ready self-control.

"It was rather a rash promise, I am afraid."

Her voice sounded half shy and wholly sweet, and again he was caught by that elusive quality about her that had puzzled him before. It was stronger than ever, so strong that he felt for a moment on the verge of discovery. But yet again it baffled him, making him all the more determined to pursue it to its source.

"You're not going to cry off?" he said, with a smile.

He saw her flush behind her mask.

"Only with your permission," she answered.

He heard the note of pleading in her voice, but he would not notice it.

"Oh, I can't let you off!" he said lightly. "Gwen would never forgive me. Besides, I don't want to."

She said no more, probably realising that he meant to have his way. They talked upon indifferent topics in the midst of the general buzz of merriment till, supper over, they separated.

"I shall come for that midnight dance," were Carey's last words, as he bowed and left her.

And during the hour that intervened he kept a sharp eye upon her, lest her evident reluctance to remain should prove too much for her integrity. He was half amused at his own tenacity in the matter. Not for years had a chance acquaintance so excited his curiosity.

A few minutes

before midnight he was standing before her. The last dance of the evening had just begun. Gwen had decreed that everyone should stop upon the stroke of twelve, while every mask was removed, after which the dance was to be continued to the finish.

"Shall we go upstairs?" suggested

Carey.

To his surprise he felt
that the hand she
laid upon his arm was
trembling.

"By all means," she
answered. "Let us
get away from the
crowd!"

It was an unexpected
request, but he
showed no surprise.
He piloted her to a

secluded spot in the upper regions, and they sat down on a lounge at the end of a corridor.

A queer sense of uneasiness had begun to oppress Carey, as strong as it was inexplicable. He made a resolute effort to ignore it. The music downstairs was sinking away. He took out his watch.

"The dramatic moment approaches," he remarked, after a pause. "Are you ready?"

She did not speak.

"I'll tell you why I want to see you unmask," he said, speaking very quietly. "It is because there is something about you that reminds me of someone I know, but the resemblance is so subtle that it has eluded me all the evening."

"You do not know me," she said. And he felt that she spoke with an effort.

"I am not so sure," he answered. "But in any case—"

He paused. The music had ceased altogether,

and an expectant
silence prevailed. He
looked at her intently
as he waited, till
aware that she shrank
from his scrutiny.

A long deep note
boomed through
the house, echoing
weirdly through
the intense silence.
Carey put up his hand
without speaking, and
stripped off his mask.
He crumpled it into

a ball as the second
note struck, and
looked at her. She had
not moved. He waited
silently.

At the sixth note
she made a sudden,
almost passionate
gesture and rose.
Carey remained
motionless, watching
her. Swiftly she
turned, and began to
walk away from him.
He leaned forward. His

eyes were fixed upon her.

Three more strokes! She stopped abruptly, turning back as if he had spoken. Moving slowly, and still masked, she came back to him. He met her under a lamp. His face was very pale, but his eyes were steady and piercingly keen. He took her hand, bending over it till his lips touched her glove.

"I know you now," he said, his voice very low.

Three more strokes, and silence.

A ripple of laughter suddenly ran through the house, a gay voice called for three cheers, and as though a spell had been lifted the merriment burst out afresh in tune to the lilting dance-music.

Carey straightened himself slowly, still holding the slender hand in his. Her mask had gone at last, and he stood face to face with the woman of his dream—the woman whose hard-won security he had only that morning pledged himself to shatter.

VII

"You know me," she said.

"Yes; I know you. And I know your secret, too."

The words sounded stern. He was putting strong restraint upon himself.

She faced him without flinching, her look as steady as his own. And yet again it was to Carey as though he stood in the presence of a queen. She did not say a word.

"Will you believe me," he said slowly, "when I tell you that I would give all I have not to know it?"

She raised her

beautiful brows for a moment, but still she said nothing.

He let her hand go. "I was on the point of searching to the world's end for you," he said. "But since I have found you here of all places, I am bound to take advantage of it. Forgive me, if you can!"

He saw a gleam of apprehension in her eyes.

"What is it you want to say to me?" she asked.

He passed the question by.

"You know me, I suppose?"

She bent her head.

"I fancied it was you from the first. When I saw your hand at supper, I knew."

"And you tried to avoid me?"

"When you have something to conceal, it is wise to avoid anyone connected with it."

She answered him very quietly, but he

knew instinctively that she was fighting him with her whole strength. It was almost more than he could bear.

"Believe me," he said, "I am not a man to wantonly betray a woman's secret. I have kept yours faithfully for years. But when within the last few days I came to know who you were, and that your husband, Major Coningsby, was contemplating making a second marriage, I was in honour bound to speak."

"You told him?" She raised her eyes for a single instant, and he read in them a reproach unutterable.

His heart smote him. What had she

endured, this woman, before taking that final step to cut herself off from the man whose name she had borne? But he would not yield an inch. He was goaded by pitiless necessity.

"I told him," he answered. "But I had no means of proving what I said. And he refused to believe me."

"And now?" she almost whispered.

He heard the note of tragedy in the words, and he braced himself to meet her most desperate resistance.

"Before I go further," he said, "let me tell you this! Slight though you may consider our acquaintance to be, I have always felt—I have always known—that you are a good woman."

She made a quick gesture of protest.

"Would a good woman have left the man who saved her life lying ill in a strange land while she escaped with her miserable freedom?"

He answered her without hesitation,

as he had long ago answered himself.

"No doubt the need was great."

She turned away from him and sat down, bowing her head upon her hand.

"It was," she said, her voice very low. "I was nearly mad with trouble. You had pity then—without

knowing. Have you—
no pity—now?"

The appeal went out
into silence. Carey
neither spoke nor
moved. His face was
like a stone mask—
the face of a strong
man in torture.

After a pause of
seconds she spoke
again, her face hidden
from him.

"The first Mrs. Coningsby is dead," she said. "Let it be so! Nothing will ever bring her back. Geoffrey Coningsby is free to marry—whom he will."

The words were scarcely more than a whisper, but they reached and pierced him to the heart. He drew a step nearer to her, and spoke with sudden vehemence.

"I would help you, Heaven knows, if I could! But you will see—you must see presently—that I have no choice. There is only one thing to be done, and it has fallen to me to see it through, though it would be easier for me to die!"

He broke off. There was strangled passion in his voice. Abruptly he turned his back upon her, and began to pace up and down. Again there fell a long pause. The music and the tramp of dancing feet below rose up in his ears like a shout of mockery. He was fighting the hardest battle of his life, fighting single-handed and grievously wounded for a victory that would cripple him for the rest of his days.

Suddenly he stood still and looked at her, though she had not moved, unless her head with its silvery hair were bowed a little lower than before. For a single instant he hesitated, then strode impulsively to her, and knelt down by her side.

"God help us both!" he said hoarsely.

His hands were on her shoulders. He drew her to him, taking the bowed head upon his breast. And so, silently, he held her. When she looked up at last, he knew that the bitter triumph was his. Her face was deathly, but her eyes were steadfast. She drew herself very gently out of his hold.

"I do not think," she said, "that there is anyone else in the world who could have done for me what you have done tonight." She paused a moment looking straight into his eyes, then laid her hands in his without a quiver. "Years ago," she said, "you saved my life. Tonight—you have saved something infinitely more precious than that. And I—I am grateful to you. I will do— whatever you think right."

It was a free surrender, but it wrung his heart to accept it. Even in that moment of tragedy there was to him something of that sublime courage with which she had faced the tumult of a stormy sea with him five years before. And very poignantly it came home to him that he was there to destroy and not to deliver. Like a wave of evil, it rushed upon him, overwhelming him.

He could not trust himself to speak. The wild words that ran in his brain were such as he could not utter. And so he only bent his head once more over the hands that lay so trustingly in his, and with great reverence he kissed them.

VIII

It was on a cold, dark evening two days later that Major Coningsby returned from the first run of the year, and tramped, mud-splashed and stiff from hard riding, into his gloomy house. A gust of rain blew swirling after him, and he turned, swearing, and shut the great door with a bang. It had not been a good day for sport. The ground had been sodden, and the scent had washed away. He had followed the hounds for miles to no purpose and had galloped home at last in sheer disgust. To add to his grievances he had called upon Lady Emberdale on his way back, and had not found her in. "Gone to tea with her precious Admiral, I suppose!" he had growled, as he rode away, which, as it chanced, was the case. The suspicion had not improved his mood, and he was very much out of humour when he finally reached his own domain. Striding into the library, he turned on the threshold to curse his servant for not having lighted the lamp, and the man hastened forward nervously to repair the omission. This accomplished, he as hastily retired, glancing furtively over his shoulder as he made his escape.

Coningsby tramped to the hearth, and stood there, beating his leg irritably with his riding-whip. There was a heavy frown on his face. He did not once raise his eyes to the picture above him. He was still thinking of Lady Emberdale and the Admiral. Finally, with a sudden idea of refreshing himself, he wheeled towards the table. The next instant, he stood and stared as if transfixed.

A woman dressed in black, and thickly veiled, was standing facing him under the lamp.

He gazed at her speechlessly for a second or two,

then passed his hand across his eyes.

"Great heavens!" he said slowly, at last.

She made a quick movement of the hands that was like a gesture of shrinking.

"You don't know me?" she asked, in a voice so low as to be barely audible.

For a moment there flashed into his face the curious, listening look that is seen on the faces of the blind. Then violently he strode forward.

"I should know that voice in ten thousand!" he cried, his words sharp and quivering. "Take off your veil, woman! Show me your face!"

The hunger in his eyes was terrible to see. He looked like a dying man reaching out impotent hands for some priceless elixir of life.

"Your face!" he gasped again hoarsely, brokenly. "Show me your face!"

Mutely she obeyed him, removed hat and veil with fingers that never faltered, and turned her sad, calm face towards him. For seconds longer he stared at her, stared devouringly, fiercely, with the eyes of a madman. Then, suddenly, with a great cry, he stumbled forward, flinging himself upon his knees at the table, with his face hidden on his arms.

"Oh, I know you! I know you!" he sobbed. "You've tortured me like this before. You've made me think I had only to open my arms to you, and I should have you close against my heart. It's happened night after night, night after night! Naomi! Naomi! Naomi!"

His voice choked, and he became intensely

still crouching there
before her in an
anguish too great for
words.

For a long time she
was motionless too,
but at last, as he did
not move, she came
a step toward him,
pity and repugnance
struggling visibly for
the mastery over
her. Reluctantly she
stooped and touched
his shoulder.

"Geoffrey!" she said, "it is I, myself, this time."

He started at her touch but did not lift his head.

She waited, and presently he began to recover himself. At last he blundered heavily to his feet.

"It's true, is it?" he said, peering at her

uncertainly. "You're here—in the flesh? You've been having just a ghastly sort of game with me all these years, have you? Hang it, I didn't deserve quite that! And so the little newspaper chap spoke the truth, after all."

He paused; then suddenly flung out his arms to her as he

stood.

"Naomi!" he cried, "come to me, my girl! Don't be afraid. I swear I'll be good to you, and I'm a man that keeps his oath! Come to me, I say!"

But she held back from him, her face still white and calm.

"No, Geoffrey," she said very firmly, "I

haven't come back to you for that. When I left you, I left you for good. And you know why. I never meant to see your face again. You had made my life with you impossible. I have only come to-day as—as a matter of principle, because I heard you were going to marry again."

The man's arms fell

slowly.

"You were always rather great on principle," he said, in an odd tone.

He was not angry— that she saw. But the sudden dying away of the eagerness on his face made him look old and different. This was not the man whose hurricanes of violence had once overwhelmed her, whose unrestrained passions had finally driven her from him to take refuge in a lie.

"I should not have come," she said, speaking with less assurance, "if it had not been to prevent a wrong being done to another woman."

His expression did not

change.

"I see," he said quietly. "Who sent you? Carey?"

She flushed uncontrollably at the question, though there was no offence in the tone in which it was uttered.

"Yes," she answered, after a moment.

Coningsby turned slowly and looked into the fire.

"And how did he persuade you?" he asked. "Did he tell you I was going blind?"

"No!" There was apprehension as well as surprise in her voice; and he jerked his head up as though listening to it.

"Ah, well!" he said. "It doesn't much matter. There is a remedy for all this world's evils. No doubt I shall take it sooner or later. So you're going again are you? I'm not to touch you; not to kiss your hand? You won't have me as husband, slave, or dog! Egad!" He laughed out harshly. "I used not to be so humble. If you were queen, I was king, and I made you know it. There! Go! You have done what you came to do, and more also. Go quickly, before I see your face again! I'm only mortal still, and there are some things that mortals can't endure—even strong men—even giants. So—good-bye!"

He stopped abruptly. He was gripping the

high mantelpiece with both hands. Every bone of them stood out distinctly, and the veins shone purple in the lamplight. His head was bowed forward upon his chest. He was fighting fiercely with that demon of unfettered violence to which he had yielded such complete allegiance all his life.

Minutes passed. He

dared not turn his head to look but he knew that she had not gone. He waited dumbly, still forcing back the evil impulse that tore at his heart. But the tension became at last intolerable, and slowly, still gripping himself with all his waning strength, he stood up and turned.

She was standing

close to him. The repugnance had all gone out of her face. It held only the tenderness of a great compassion.

As he stared at her dumbfounded, she held out her hands to him.

"Geoffrey," she said, "if you wish it, I will come back to you."

He stared at her, still wide-eyed and mute, as though a spell were upon him.

"Won't you have me, Geoffrey?" she said, a faint quiver in her voice.

He seized her hands then, seized them, and drew her to him, bowing his head down upon her shoulder with a great sob.

"Naomi, Naomi," he whispered huskily, "I will be good to you, my darling—so help me, God!"

Her own eyes were full of tears. She yielded herself to him without a word.

IX

"Can I come in a moment, Reggie?"

Gwen's bright face peered round the door at him as he sat at the writing-table in his room, with his head upon his hand. He looked up at her.

"Yes, come in, child! What is it?"

She entered eagerly and went to him.

"Are you busy, dear old boy? It is horrid

that you should be going away so soon. I only wanted just to tell you something that the dear old Admiral has just told me."

She sat down in her favourite position on the arm of his chair, her arm about his neck. Her eyes were shining. Carey looked up at her.

"Well?" he said. "Has he plucked up courage at last to ask for what he wants?"

"Yes; he actually has." There was a purr of content in Gwen's voice. "And it's quite all right, Reggie. Mummy has said 'yes,' as I knew she would, directly I told her about Major Coningsby finding his wife again. All she said to that was: 'Dear me! How annoying for poor Major Coningsby!' I thought it was horrid of her to say that, but I didn't say so, for I wanted it all to come quite casually. And after that I wrote to Charlie, and he told the Admiral. And he came straight over only this morning and asked her. He's been telling me all about it, and he's so awfully happy! He says he was a big fool not to ask her long ago in the summer. For what do you think she said, Reggie, when he told her that he'd been wanting to marry her for ever so long, but couldn't be quite sure how she felt about it? Why, she said, with that funny little laugh of hers—you know her way—'My dear Admiral, I was only waiting to be asked.' The dear old man nearly cried when he told me. And I kissed him. And he and Charlie are coming over to dine this evening. So we can all be happy together."

Gwen paused to breathe, and to give her cousin an ardent hug.

"You've been a

perfect dear about it," she ended with enthusiasm. "It would never have happened but for you, and—and Mademoiselle Trèves. Do you think she hated going back to that man very badly?"

"I think she did," said Carey.

He was looking, not at Gwen, but straight

at the window in front of him. There were deep lines about his eyes, as if he had not slept of late.

"But she needn't have stayed," urged Gwen.

He did not answer. In his pocket there lay a slip of paper containing a few brief lines in a woman's hand.

"I have taken up my burden again, and, God helping me, I will carry it now to the end. You know what it means to me, but I shall always thank you in my heart, because in the hour of my utter weakness you were strong.— NAOMI CONINGSBY."

The splendid courage that underlay those few words had not

hidden from the man the cost of her sacrifice. She had gone voluntarily back into the bondage that once had crushed her to the earth. And he—and he only—knew what it meant to her.

He was brought back to his surroundings by the pressure of Gwen's arm. He turned and found her looking closely into his face.

"Reggie," she said, with a touch of shyness, "are you—unhappy—about something?" He did not answer her at once, and she slipped suddenly down upon her knees by his side. "Forgive me, dear old boy! Do you know, I couldn't help guessing a little? You're not vexed?"

He laid a silencing

hand upon her shoulder.

"I don't mind your knowing, dear," he said gently.

And he stooped, and kissed her forehead. She clung to him closely for a second. When she rose, her eyes were wet. But, obedient to his unspoken desire, she did not say another word.

When she was gone Carey roused himself from his preoccupation, and concentrated his thoughts upon his correspondence. He was leaving England in two days, and travelling to the East on a solitary shooting expedition. He did not review the prospect with much relish, but inaction had become intolerable to him, and he had an intense longing to get away. He had arranged to return to town that afternoon.

It was towards luncheon-time that he left his room, and, descending, came upon Lady Emberdale in the hall. She turned to meet him, a slight flush upon her face.

"No doubt Gwen has told you our piece of news?" she said.

He held out his hand.

"It is official, is it? I am very glad. I wish you joy with all my heart."

She accepted his congratulations with a gracious smile.

"I think everyone

is pleased, including those absurd children. By the way, here is a note just come for you, brought by a groom from Crooklands Manor. I was going to bring it up to you, as he is waiting for an answer."

He took it up and opened it hastily, with a murmured excuse. When he looked up,

Lady Emberdale saw at once that there was something wrong. She began to question him, but he held the note out to her with a quick gesture, and she took it from him.

"My husband met with an accident while motoring this morning," she read. "He has been brought home, terribly injured, and keeps asking for you. Can you come?

"N. CONINGSBY."

Glancing up, she saw Carey, pale and stern, waiting to speak.

"Send back word, 'Yes, at once,'" he said. "And perhaps you can spare me the car?"

He turned away without waiting for

her reply, and went back to his room, crushing the note unconsciously in his hand.

X

"And the sea—gave up—the dead—that were in it." Haltingly the words fell through the silence. There was a certain monotony about them, as if they had been often repeated. The speaker turned his head from side to side upon the pillow uneasily, as if conscious of restraint, then spoke again in the tone of one newly awakened. "Why doesn't that fellow come?" he demanded restlessly. "Did you tell him I couldn't wait?"

"He is coming," a quiet voice answered at his side. "He will soon be here."

He moved his head again at the words, seeming to listen intently.

"Ah, Naomi, my girl," he said, "you've turned up trumps at last. It won't have been such a desperate sacrifice after all, eh, dear? It's wonderful how things get squared. Is that the doctor there? I can't see very well."

The doctor bent over him.

"Are you wanting anything?"

"Nothing—nothing, except that fellow Carey. Why in thunder doesn't he come? No;

there's nothing you can do. I'm pegging out. My time is up. You can't put back the clock. I wouldn't let you if you could—not as things are. I have been a blackguard in my time, but I'll take my last hedge straight. I'll die like a man."

Again he turned his head, seeming to listen.

"I thought I heard something. Did someone open the door? It's getting very dark."

Yes; the door had opened, but only the dying brain had caught the sound. As Carey came noiselessly forward only the dying man greeted him.

"Ah, here you are! Come quite close to

me! I want to see you, if I can. You're the little newspaper chap who saved my life at Magersfontein?"

"Yes," Carey said.

He sat down by Coningsby's side, facing the light.

"I was told you wanted me," he said.

"Yes; I want you to

give me a promise." Coningsby spoke rapidly, with brows drawn together. "I suppose you know I'm a dead man?"

"I don't believe in death," Carey answered very quietly.

Coningsby's eyes burned with a strange light.

"Nor I," he said. "Nor

I. I've been too near it before now to be afraid. Also, I've lived too long and too hard to care overmuch for what is left. But there's one thing I mean to do before I go. And you'll give me your promise to see it through?"

He paused, breathing quick and short; then went on hurriedly, as a man whose time is limited.

"You'll stick to it, I know, for you're a fellow that speaks the truth. I nearly thrashed you for it, once. Remember? You said I wasn't fit for the society of any good woman. And you were right—quite right. I never have been. Yet you ended by sending me the best woman in the world. What made you do that, I wonder?"

Carey did not answer. His face was sternly composed. He had not once glanced at the woman who sat on the other side of Coningsby's bed.

Coningsby went on unheeding.

"I drove her away from me, and

you—you sent her back. I don't think I could have done that for the woman I loved. For you do love her, eh, Carey? I remember seeing it in your face that first night I brought you here. It comes back to me. You were standing before her portrait in the library. You didn't know I saw you. I was drunk at the time. But I've remembered it since."

Again he paused.
His breath was
slowing down. It
came spasmodically,
with long silences
between.

Carey had listened
with his eyes fixed
and hard, staring
straight before him,
but now slowly at
length he turned his
head, and looked

down at the man who was dying.

"Hadn't you better tell me what it is you want me to do?" he said.

"Ah!" Coningsby seemed to rouse himself. "It isn't much, after all," he said. "I made my will only this morning. It was on my way back that I had the smash. I was quite sober, only I couldn't see very well, and I lost control. All my property goes to my wife. That's all settled. But there's one thing left—one thing left—which I am going to leave you. It's the only thing I value, but there's no nobility about it, for I can't take it with me where I'm going. I want you, Carey—when I'm dead—to marry the woman you love, and give her happiness. Don't wait for the sake of decency! That consideration never appealed to me. I say it in her presence, that she may know it is my wish. Marry her, man—you love each other—did you think I didn't know? And take her away to some Utopia of your own, and—and—teach her—to forget me."

His voice shook and ceased. His wife had slipped to her knees by the bed, hiding her face. Carey sat mute and motionless, but the grim look had passed from his face. It was almost tender.

Gaspingly at length Coningsby spoke again: "Are you going to do it, Carey? Are you going to give me your promise? I shall sleep the easier for it."

Carey turned to him and gripped one of the man's powerless hands in his own. For a moment he did not speak—it almost seemed he could not. Then at last, very low, but resolute his answer came:

"I promise to do my part," he said.

In the silence that followed he rose noiselessly and moved away.

He left Naomi still kneeling beside the bed, and as he passed out he heard the dying man speak her name. But what passed between them he never knew.

When he saw her again, nearly an

hour later, Geoffrey Coningsby was dead.

XI

It was on a day of frosty sunshine, nearly a fortnight later, that Carey dismounted before the door of Crooklands Manor, and asked for its mistress.

He was shown at once

into the library, where he found her seated before a great oak bureau with a litter of papers all around her.

She flushed deeply as she rose to greet him. They had not met since the day of her husband's funeral.

"I see you're busy," he said, as he came forward.

"Yes," she assented. "Such stacks of papers that must be examined before they can be destroyed. It's dreary work, and I have been very thankful to have Gwen with me. She has just gone out riding."

"I met her," Carey said. "She was with young Rivers."

"It is a farewell ride,"

Naomi told him. "She goes back to school to-morrow. Dear child! I shall miss her. Please sit down!"

The colour had ebbed from her face, leaving it very pale. She did not look at Carey, but began slowly to sort afresh a pile of correspondence.

He ignored her request, and stood

watching her till
at last she laid the
packet down.

Then somewhat
abruptly he spoke:
"I've just come in to
tell you my plans."

"Yes?" She took up an
old cheque-book, as
if she could not bear
to be idle, and began
to look through it,
seeming to search for
something.

Again he fell silent, watching her.

"Yes?" she repeated after a moment, bending a little over the book she held.

"They are very simple," he said quietly. "I'm going to a place I know of in the Himalayas where there is a wonderful river that one can punt along all day and all night, and never come to an end."

Again he paused. The fingers that held the memorandum were not quite steady.

"And you have come to say good-bye?" she suggested in her deep, sad voice.

His eyes were turned gravely upon her, but there was a faint smile at the corners of his mouth.

"No," he said in his abrupt fashion. "That isn't in the plan. Good-bye to the rest of the world if you will, but never again to you!"

He drew close to her and gently took the cheque-book out of her grasp.

"I want you to come with me, Naomi," he said very tenderly. "My darling, will you come? I have wanted you—for years."

A great quiver went through her, as though every pulse leapt to the words he uttered. For a second she stood quite still, with her face lifted to the sunlight. Then she turned, without question or words of any sort, as she had turned long ago—yet with a difference— and laid her hand with perfect confidence in his.

THE END

ABOUT THE AUTHOR

Ethel M. Dell has delighted millions around the world with her best selling stories of love and longing. A shy and private person, she was forty when she married the love her life, a solider named Gerald Tahourdin Savage. This story was first published in 1920.

ABOUT THE COVER

The cover is adapted from a poster for the 1939 movie starring Heddy Lemar, 'Lady of the Tropics,' and the background is a painting by Winslow Homer called 'Early Morning After a Storm at Sea.'

MORE TITLES AVAILABLE IN SUPER LARGE PRINT

* **The Bohemian Girl** *
Willa Cather

* **The Diamond as Big as the Ritz** *
F. Scott Fitzgerald

* **Man with Two Left Feet** *
P.G. Wodehouse

* **Little Daylight** *

WESTERNS
ROMANCES
ADVENTURE
MYSTERIES
THRILLERS
HORROR
SCIENCE FICTION
FANTASY
POETRY
HISTORY
HUMOR
BIOGRAPHIES
MEMOIRS

it's all available in...
SUPER LARGE PRINT

MORE BOOKS AT:
superlargeprint.com

KEEP ON READING!

This book is set in a font designed by
Abelardo Gonzalez called OpenDyslexic.

ISBN 154860481X
ISBN 978-1548604813

Printed in Great Britain
by Amazon